Oh, Barbara... Get It Together!

A Tale of Pants Battles, Heel Hate, and Surprise Kicks

Lacey Hill-Joga
& Deedra Abboud

ISBN: 978-1-956565-52-2

Lacey is a retired U.S. Army veteran who swapped combat boots for paintbrushes and a beautifully chaotic life stitched together with homeschool schedules, endless doctor's appointments, and spontaneous kitchen dance parties—courtesy of Barbara, her misbehaving left leg.

Diagnosed with Lyme disease in 2009 and multiple sclerosis soon after, Lacey now channels her creativity and resilience into art, storytelling, and homeschooling her two curious, lively daughters alongside her husband George—a Navy man with Army roots.

The Barbara Chronicles is Lacey's children's book series chronicling her funny, heartfelt journey through MS—with one rebellious leg and a few other uncooperative roommates.

Follow Lacey's journey—one story, one smile, one step at a time.

NopeDaysLife@gmail.com

In the whimsical land of Lanie-Lou—
where Laundry Mountain towers beside
Great Couch Plains and even the fridge
has opinions—lived a very peculiar
companion named Barbara.

She wasn't a cat.
She wasn't a gnome.
She wasn't even a particularly
naughty toddler.

Barbara was Lanie's left leg.
A very dramatic left leg.

A left leg with multiple sclerosis—
and a lot of feelings.

Barbara did not enjoy mornings.
Or pants.
Or structure.

Which is why, one Tuesday morning, when Lanie tried to put her pants on, Barbara refused to cooperate.

"Left leg in," Lanie said, balancing carefully while holding her jeans.

She raised Barbara—slowly, gently— toward the pants leg.

Barbara immediately twisted, flailed, and then went stiff like a grumpy raccoon caught in a sweater.

"Oh, Barbara," Lanie said.
"Come on. Get it together."

Barbara didn't get it together.

She got worse.

After two more attempts, one hopping
disaster, and a brief conversation with
gravity, Lanie flopped onto the bed.

She held her jeans open and spoke in her calmest, most serious Mom voice.

"We are going to get into these pants." she told her leg.

Barbara twitched.

"Do not start with me," Lanie whispered.

"You want me to cancel the scooter ride? I'm not above threats."

Barbara shivered slightly.

And finally—finally—Lanie managed to guide Barbara into the pants leg like threading a noodle into a keyhole.

"Victory!" she exclaimed.

Barbara immediately slumped like a bored teenager.

Later that week,
Lanie faced a new challenge:
navigating the living room jungle.

Bina and Gigi, ages seven and nine, were
lying on the floor watching cartoons with
the intensity of philosophers.

Their heads were on pillows.
Their feet were all over the place.
Their bodies were perfectly in the way.

Lanie approached with caution.
"I'm going to step over you," she warned.

"Nobody move. Especially Barbara."

She stepped carefully with her right leg,
lifting it over Gigi.

And just as she went to follow with her left
–
WHACK.

Barbara flung herself sideways
like a sleepy goat.

"Ow!" Gigi cried, grabbing her shoulder.

"Oh my gosh, are you okay?" Lanie gasped.

"That was Barbara, not me! I swear!"

Gigi blinked at her.
"Oh, Barbara. Get it together."

It happened again a few days later—
this time, Bina was the victim.

Barbara did not step.

She kicked.

Bina glared at Lanie.
"Which leg is Barbara again?"

"The left," Lanie said, trying not to panic.

Without a word, Bina walked up,
reared back, and punched
Lanie's left leg with all her
seven-year-old might.

"TAKE THAT, BARBARA!"

Lanie gasped. "Bina!"

Bina crossed her arms.
"That was self-defense."

And then came The High Heel Incident.

Lanie was getting ready for a nice dinner.

The girls were playing dress-up.

Ramon was on kid-wrangling duty.

And Lanie?

Lanie was determined to look cute.

She hadn't worn heels in months.
But tonight felt like a "try again" night.
She stepped into the right heel.

No problem.

She raised her left leg—Barbara—and
hovered above the second shoe.

Barbara twitched.

Lanie narrowed her eyes.
"We are going to do this."

She lowered her heel.

Barbara collapsed like overcooked spaghetti.

Lanie barely caught herself on the dresser.

"Okay," she said calmly, setting the shoes aside. "Message received."

Five minutes later, Lanie rolled out of the garage on her red scooter, stylish flats on her feet and sparkles in her hair.

Barbara, notably, behaved the entire evening.

As the sun set on another chaotic, wonderful week in Lanie-Lou, Lanie sat on the porch with a cold drink, watching Bina and Gigi chase fireflies through the yard.

Barbara rested quietly—tired but calm.

"She's not all bad," Lanie said to no one in particular.

"She just has... ideas."

Barbara still kicks.
She flails.

She fights pants, hates high heels, and
sometimes clocks a kid without warning.

But she's also taught us how to laugh,
how to slow down, and how to keep going—
one wobbly step at a time.

Because even when life doesn't cooperate,
you can still put your pants on.
Eventually.

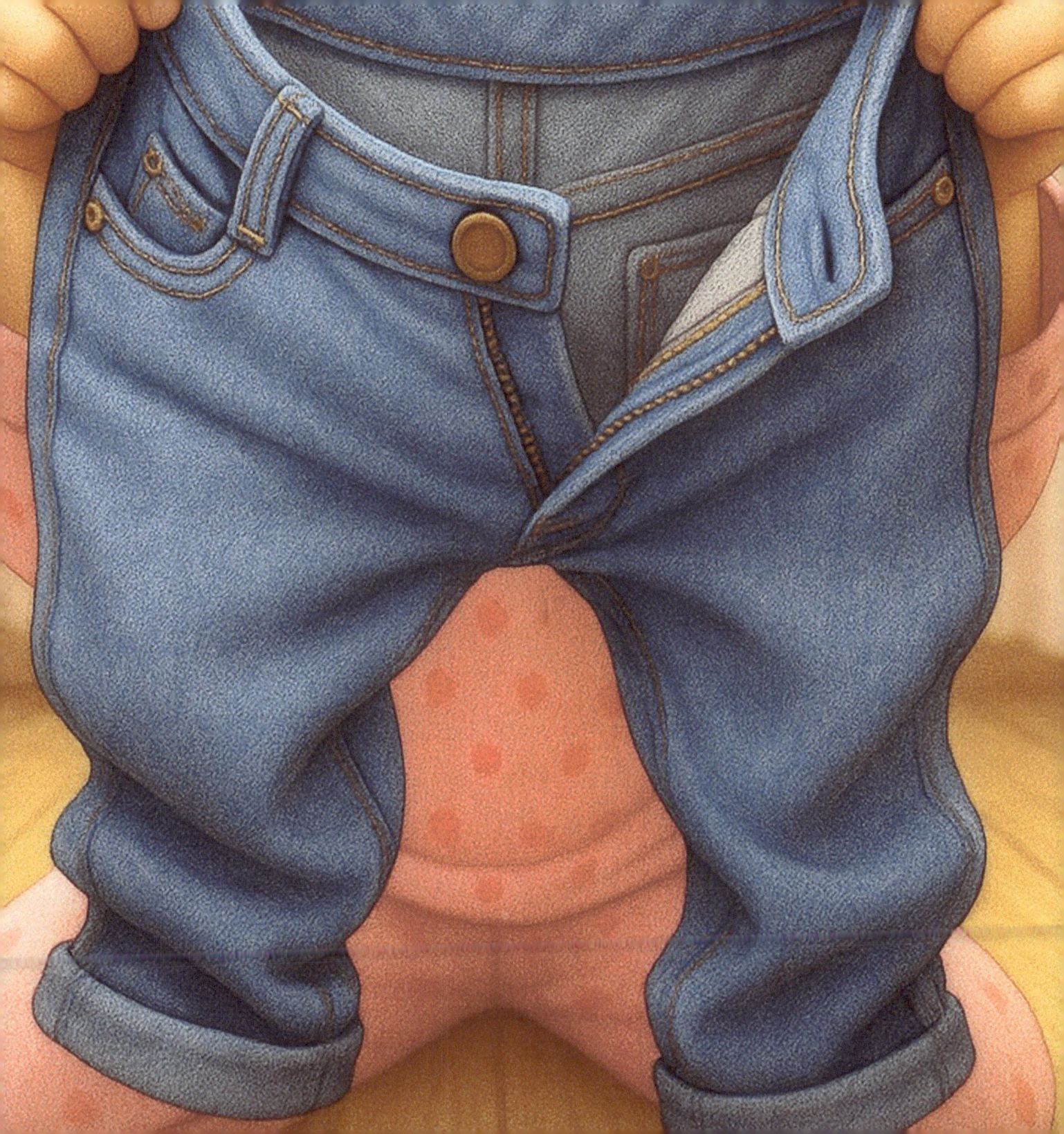

If you *enjoyed* this book,
we'd be so *grateful* if you'd share the
love by leaving a *review* on Amazon!

More from the "Barbara Chronicles" Series:

Whoa There, Barbara!

Barbara and The Grocery Train Adventure
(Coming soon) *Barbara & the Couch Kingdom*
(Coming soon) *Barbara & The Stairway Struggle*
(Coming soon) *Barbara & the Birthday Balloon Incident*